NICOLA DAVIES
THE EEL QUESTION

ILLUSTRATIONS BETH HOLLAND

*For Simon Barnes, who knows about the
surprises of a flat landscape.*

The Eel Question
Published in Great Britain in 2018
by Graffeg Limited.

Written by Nicola Davies
copyright © 2018.
Illustrated by Beth Holland
copyright © 2018.
Designed and produced by Graffeg
Limited copyright © 2018.

Graffeg Limited, 24 Stradey Park
Business Centre, Mwrwg Road,
Llangennech, Llanelli, Carmarthenshire
SA14 8YP Wales UK
Tel 01554 824000 www.graffeg.com

ISBN 9781910862520

1 2 3 4 5 6 7 8 9

NICOLA DAVIES
THE EEL QUESTION

ILLUSTRATIONS BETH HOLLAND

GRAFFEG

THE EEL QUESTION

Everything about a hilly landscape invites curiosity. What lies at the end of that valley? What could be beyond that ridge? Even the water in the hills is always on its way to somewhere else, suggesting the possibility of other places, other ways to be. In the hills, you can see from where you are, to where you might be.

But a flat landscape squashes enquiry. The horizon closes in and what lies beyond it is unknown and unknowable. The water is lazy, reluctant to go anywhere. Here is where you are, a flat land says, here is all that matters; here is all there is.

Nant lived in a flat landscape, the flattest of all, a marsh. A maze of stagnant pools and reed beds spread out in all directions from anywhere she had ever stood. The horizon was usually close enough to touch, and the only comment that the marsh ever made was an eternal shushing.

Yet, somehow Nant had been born with the questioning soul of an uplander. What and why, how and when, were almost always on her lips. This in spite of the fact that questions only ever earned her blows from her master, Dith, who was a marsh man through and through and didn't hold with any kind of curiosity.

How Nant had come to be in Dith's service no one had bothered to note and Nant had been too young to remember. Probably just a child born at the wrong time, to a family already burdened with hungry mouths, and sold as soon as she was weaned. It was the one topic that Nant no longer asked about. But she seemed unable to stop asking about almost everything else, and had long accepted that her face would be a variety of colours, from vivid purple to fading yellow, the diary of her enquiries and of Dith's irritation with them.

There were times when it was safer to ask

questions than others. Hauling eel traps in an east wind was one. In these conditions, the job took two pairs of hands. Nant's, as usual, were set to the task with the least skill, the only tasks Dith said she was fit for. So she steadied the flat-bottomed punt while Dith pulled the traps from the water with a silence and solemnity that suggested a religious ritual. This meant that Nant was at one end of the boat while Dith was entirely occupied at the other, putting her safely beyond the reach of her master's fists.

Dith pulled the eels from the trap and bashed their heads on the gunwale; the only eel that would not find its way back to the water was a dead one. He dropped the heavy bodies into the willow creel and they shone through the weave. These were not ordinary eels, brown as mud with eyes like an apple pip, but the first silvers of the season, the colour of moonlight, with huge, round eyes, like fallen stars.

"Where do they come from, the silvers?"

It was the question Nant asked every autumn when the rains came and silvers filled the traps from one moon to the next, then disappeared until the next year. Dith grunted. It was as much of an answer as she expected to any of her questions. It didn't matter. What mattered was the asking; it helped her to hold her shape against the whispering nothing of the reeds that every day seemed to make her flatter.

"And where do they go?" Nant breathed, "Where do they go?" That was the part that really fascinated her. "Where could these moonlight serpents go?"

Nant felt in her soul that the eels' disappearance meant something, that it held a message about the nature of the world and what was in it, if only she could work out what.

Nant's next question burst from her mouth loud and clear.

"What's that?"

The eel catcher's attention was distracted from his trap. He scowled at Nant and was about to promise her another bruise, but her face made him look to where she pointed. Up ahead, where the channel gleamed in the grey dawn light, a line of shining curves was porpoising towards the far bank.

"It's the King of the Eels, Dith!" Nant exclaimed, "He's coming to claim his kingdom!"

The story of the giant Eel King was told around every fire: he would come to rescue his people while humanity had to fend for itself in fire or flood, or whatever the last apocalypse proved to be. Nant felt a thrill pass through her; the world's end would at least be a change.

Dith snorted in contempt and spat into the water into which the mythic creature had just vanished.

"Ain't no giant eel," he snarled, "don't you know a bitch otter and her cubs when you see 'em?"

He sat down in the prow and pulled the next trap from the pile.

"Thems is wicked enough without monster eels," he snarled. "They'll be stealing my silvers. If I catch 'em, I'll skin 'em alive. Now get this punt moved, we got twenty more traps to haul."

Nant pushed the punt along the channel. She sniffed the wind. For days now it had carried a strange smell, a whiff of burning not like a regular fire, that made her skin prickle with fear. Every day it grew stronger, but when she'd asked Dith what it was, she'd earned a split lip which had only just scabbed over. So, now, Nant held her tongue and thought instead about the King of the Eels. Dith was right, of course, about the otter family. But what was an otter thinking to have a litter so late in the year, when the reeds had already turned brown? Was that something else, like the silvers and the scent in the wind, that held a message she couldn't read?

The sun showed, pale over the reeds as they

reached the last trap. Dith grunted as he tried to pull it from the water and failed.

"Get here!" he growled, "Trap's caught on somethin'."

The wind had dropped, so the punt could be held in place by wedging the pole deep into the mud. Nant joined Dith in the prow. The threat of violence came off him stronger than the stink of his oily body. If this trap could not be hauled she knew she would somehow be to blame. She reached into the water and laced her fingers into the wet weft of willow twigs.

"Lift!" Dith said.

The trap was heavy, but Nant knew instantly it was the wrong kind of heavy. There was none of the dense squirming that came with a good catch of eels. This weight was dead, and, as they got the trap into the punt, something shot out of the water, snarling, biting, clawing. It created so much chaos that it took Nant a moment to realise it was an otter. The trap had dropped to the bottom of the boat, and Dith with it. Eel catcher, eel trap and otter were now in a writhing tangle that threatened to capsize them. Dith screamed like a stuck pig, "Hit it! Hit it!"

Nant grabbed the small paddle stowed under the port side gunwale but in the whirl of fur and teeth and human limbs it was hard to see where to hit. As Dith's shrieks reached a crescendo she finally brought the paddle down with a crash. There was the unmistakeable crack of split bone, and the whirling stopped. Dith stood up, blood streaming, the dead otter grasped by the scruff. He flung the animals body over the side.

"Took your time with that paddle," he snarled.

Nant cowered, ready for the rain of blows that usually went with that kind of anger. But Dith sat down instead. His arms were ripped to ribbons and two of the fingers of his left hand were gone.

"Sort out that trap!" he ordered, "Then, get this punt home."

Dith set to binding up his wounds with strips
of rag while Nant did as she was asked. She soon
learned what the odd weight in the trap had been:
the otter's cubs. They were small enough to have
fitted down the neck of the trap in search of eels,
but too large to turn around and get out. They
had drowned. She reached in to pull them out.
The first two were cold as the water, stone dead,
but the third was warm. As Nant grasped it, it
coughed, and gave a tiny mewling cry. She pulled
it close to her body, shielding the sight and sound
of it from Dith, then she shoved it inside her
jerkin, where it would be warm next to her skin.
Why she did this, and what Dith would say about
it, were questions Nant didn't ask.

But by the time Nant tied the punt to the
jetty at the edge of the village, Dith was pale
and trembling. He left Nant to bargain with the
clamour of folk waiting to buy eels and let his
sister, Melet, help him from the punt.

"Fetch the healer!" he told her as he slammed

the door of the hut. Melet was as foul tempered as her brother and she found time to slap Nant as she passed.

"Daresay this is your doing, you little demon," she hissed.

Nant bent under the blow but otherwise took no notice. With Dith sick and Melet out of the way for the moment, she could see to the cub. She crawled into her home, a covered corner outside Dith's door made from two old fish creels, and fed the cub on sliced-up eel. Its small, leathery paws grabbed the fish eagerly and it chomped until Nant wondered if it would burst. At last it fell asleep, its belly tight against her empty one.

Over the next few days it was easy to keep out of the way when Melet or the healer or some other adult came visiting. Most of the time folk left Dith to his fate, so Nant thought it safe to play with the otter cub on the verandah outside Dith's hut, which faced away from the village and its prying eyes. She'd saved another of the silvers

to keep the cub fed and so it learned quickly to depend on her. Nant had never been trusted by anyone before. So the way the cub took food from her hands and curled comfortably against her body raised inside her a feeling so fierce, she felt she might break apart. As she watched the little creature dive in the water underneath the hut, her heart plunged into dread that it would not return. When it swam back and leapt gleefully into her lap to shake itself dry, she soared with a joy she had never known. Nant felt that all her life before the cub she had not been alive at all.

The eels she'd saved ran out, and although no slave was allowed to take out a boat alone, the fierce love for the cub overcame her terror of punishment. In the dead of night she took the punt and sat in the moon-shadow of the reeds, while eels wriggled into the trap she'd set. Poling the long boat back in the midnight stillness, she felt as if she were made of moonlight, shimmering and glinting, sparking like a star. She looked up

at the night sky and felt her mind thrill with questions. Back in her little shelter she lay awake while the cub crunched eel bones, and felt the blood rushing to every part of her body as if carrying urgent good news. At last, child and cub curled up in the old creels as the dawn broke, and slept the day round.

Loud voices and the tearing scrape of Melet's claw-like hand dragged Nant and the cub from their sleep.

"You killed him, you witch!" Melet screamed, "Dead in his bed this very evening. I saw you making evil spells, out on the mere, alone in the dark with your familiar!"

The space outside Dith's hut was crowded with people, mourning the loss of eels rather than man, and glad of a violent distraction from the sameness of a winter day.

"Witch!' they chanted gleefully, "Witch!"

Nant wrapped her arms around her middle to protect the cub but it cried out in alarm at all

the noise. At the sound, Melet screamed and the crowd gave a kind of moan.

"Where is it?" Melet screeched, "Where is that filthy thing?"

Melet grasped Nant by the hair, others grabbed her arms and legs; faces leered down at her. The cub tried to burrow into her flesh, to hide, wrapping itself in her clothing, but nothing could protect it. It fought. Bit. Drew blood, and then was thrown like a rag high in the air. It hit the edge of the jetty, slid, limp, into the water and sank.

"Drown her! Drown the witch!" the people chanted.

The crowd was one creature now, with the smell of blood in its nose. Through the ripping of her heart Nant struggled to understand why this was happening, where had this hate come from? Stretched on her back as they bound her to something, she looked up at the sky and saw an answer there: streaks of smoke and the smell of burning flesh, a distant thrum thrum thrum of drum on the air. Something was coming, and even though it was close, the villagers couldn't, wouldn't, see it. The marsh-landers could neither fight nor run, having no idea of anything that wasn't 'us' or 'here'. All they could do was find something to blame and hit out in blind fear.

The long pole they had tied her to was balanced on the fulcrum of a wooden frame, so it could be pushed out over the water and thrust below the surface. Bound, back to the wood, face to the mere, Nant looked down at the still surface, where the pure gold of sunset was reflected. There was just a second to ask why now, at her last moment, did she see that this was beautiful, before she was plunged down.

Nant felt the cold of the water invade her body and was glad of the numbing. And then, ahead of her, was a wriggle, a tell-tale twist of body, a tiny turn in the water, and then nothing. But enough for hope. If the cub had survived then there was reason for her to survive too. Nant tensed all her muscles against her bindings. She called to them the strength built up through the years of lifting and pushing a heavy punt pole, hauling traps full of eels, resisting the cold and the bruises and the smothering whispers of the reeds. *Snap* went the chords that tied her and she swam free, down and away, down and away until the breaths she took were no longer tainted with smoke and flame.

Behind her the moon had risen over the burning village. A new force had come from the east to take the flatlands. Ash and debris drifted in the water and with it Dith's punt, its mooring rope chewed through. Nant pulled herself aboard. The moonlight showed the small muddy footprints marking out the top of the gunwale. Nant's heart leapt and then fell. The cub was curled in its favourite spot, where the smell of eels was strongest just under the prow of the punt. But one look told Nant it was not alive.

Grief broke on her heart like a hard storm, with pain she never imagined possible. Why had her heart woken to life, to the joy she had felt with the cub in her arms, only for this? She crumpled, weeping, staring down into the water, wanting its blackness to take her and dissolve the pain. But there was something moving down there. Silvers. Not one, not ten, not even a thousand, but more. They were swimming in the same direction, their starry eyes fixed on the same goal. Nant gasped in wonder at the river of eels that was flowing beneath her feet, flowing west and west and west.

Inside her, the flat landscape of the marshlands was gone forever, replaced with a dark valley, and the dizzying brightness of an open hill. So many questions had no answers, but here was one answer she could find for herself. She took up the punt pole and pushed.

Nant followed the eels, through the marsh maze, down the branches of the estuary, to the blue ocean with its frame of hills and distant horizon, promising endless questions, possibilities and different ways to be.

Nicola Davies

Nicola is an award-winning author, whose many books for children include *The Day War Came*, *King of the Sky*, *LOTS*, *Tiny*, *The Promise* (winner of the 2014 English Association Picture Book award for best fiction), *A First Book of Nature* (winner of the Independent Booksellers Best Picture Book), *Whale Boy* (Blue Peter Book Awards Shortlist 2014) and the Heroes of the Wild series (Portsmouth Book Award 2014).

She graduated in Zoology, studied whales and bats and then worked for the BBC Natural History Unit. Underlying all Nicola's writing is the belief that a relationship with nature is essential to every human being, and that now, more than ever, we need to renew that relationship.

Nicola's children's books from Graffeg include *Perfect* (2017 CILIP Kate Greenaway Medal Longlist), *The Pond* (2018 CILIP Kate Greenaway Medal Longlist), the Shadows and Light series, *The Word Bird*, *Animal Surprises* and *Into the Blue*.

Beth Holland

Beth Holland is an illustrator based in Herefordshire. She is currently studying at Hereford College of Arts for a BA (hons) degree in Illustration.

From a young age, she always had a talent and hunger for both writing and drawing. She grew up as an only child which fuelled her imagination. This meant she spent her days filling pads of paper with stories, crayoned pictures of princesses, animals and most commonly dinosaurs. This creativity won her a Blue Peter badge at age seven.

This is her first book commission to launch her career as a professional illustrator. In the future, she would like to write and illustrate a children's book of her own.

Shadows and Light series

The White Hare
Nicola Davies
Illustrated by Anastasia Izlesou

Mother Cary's Butter Knife
Nicola Davies
Illustrations by Anja Uhren

Elias Martin
Nicola Davies
Illustrations by Fran Shum

The Selkie's Mate
Nicola Davies
Illustrations by Claire Jenkins

Bee Boy and the Moonflowers
Nicola Davies
Illustrations by Max Low

The Eel Question
Nicola Davies
Illustrations by Beth Holland

In the days before computers, before cars, before electricity in wires or water in taps, or food in supermarkets, before even roads and writing, people lived by what they could get from the land. Humans were closer to nature, at the mercy of the cold and wind, floods and drought, as other animals were. Back then, humans and animals were fellow beings under the sky. Perhaps that's why it seemed possible, back then, for humans to change into animals, and animals into humans.

A young woman is forced to watch helplessly as a cruel lover slays her family in pursuit of her love.

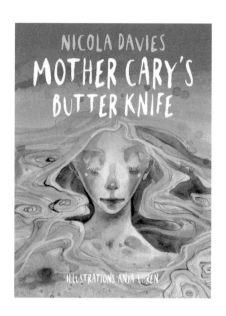

NICOLA DAVIES
MOTHER CARY'S
BUTTER KNIFE

ILLUSTRATIONS ANJA UHREN

" Out of the low slung car a tall, ancient man unfurled himself. His eyes were blue-green, like a backlit wave, his face as craggy as the coast, and topped with a tower of foam-white hair. When the man spoke, his voice was as commanding as storm waves breaking in a cave.

"The sea looks fair tonight, does it not?" he said. Keenan opened his mouth to reply but found his own voice entirely missing. The strange man growled on, and raised a warning finger before the boy's wide eyes. "

The smallest of three brothers, Keenan Mowat had a priceless talent: he loved the sea and the sea loved him right back...

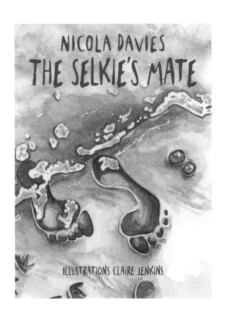

NICOLA DAVIES
THE SELKIE'S MATE

ILLUSTRATIONS CLAIRE JENKINS

In the far north-west are islands where the sea and land melt into each other in a fretwork of rocks and water. The landscape shifts from liquid to solid in little more than a step. The people who live there shift too, from making a living on land, to the ocean, and back again. Even the seals are not always seals, but sometimes selkies, beings who can slip off their skins to walk on land in human form.

In a land where people flow between ocean and land, a seal and a fisherman sing together under a glowing moon.

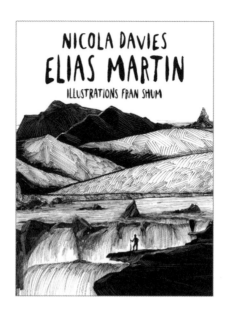

NICOLA DAVIES
ELIAS MARTIN
ILLUSTRATIONS FRAN SHUM

" By the time he washed up to the door of a one-roomed log cabin, in the remote backwoods of a northern province, he knew this was his last chance in life. He carried a fur trapper's licence, a bag of steel traps, a rifle and the conviction that all of nature was his personal enemy. He was seventeen years old. "

Trawling the north, looking for his last chance of survival, Elias Martin lives a scowling, solitary life for a decade until a small, lost child wanders into his path.

Graffeg Children's Books

The Secret of the Egg
Nicola Davies
Illustrations by Abbie Cameron

The Word Bird
Nicola Davies
Illustrations by Abbie Cameron

Animal Surprises
Nicola Davies
Illustrations by Abbie Cameron

Into the Blue
Nicola Davies
Illustrations by Abbie Cameron

Perfect
Nicola Davies
Illustrations by Cathy Fisher

Small Finds a Home
Celestine and the Hare

Paper Boat for Panda
Celestine and the Hare

Honey for Tea
Celestine and the Hare

Catching Dreams
Celestine and the Hare

A Small Song
Celestine and the Hare

Finding Your Place
Celestine and the Hare

Bertram Likes to Sew
Celestine and the Hare

Bert's Garden
Celestine and the Hare

'Life-affirming books that encourage us all
to nurture the playfulness of childhood'
Playing by the Book